Red Sings from Treetops

For Eli, who helps me see color —
and the world — in new ways.
—J.S.

For Martha.
—P.Z.

Text copyright © 2009 by Joyce Sidman
Illustrations copyright © 2009 Pamela Zagarenski

Houghton Mifflin Books for Children is an imprint of Houghton Mifflin Harcourt
Publishing Company.

www.hmhbooks.com

The text of this book is set in Oldbook ITC.
The illustrations are mixed media paintings on wood and computer illustration.

Library of Congress Cataloging-in-Publication Number 2008035947

ISBN 978-0-547-01494-4

Printed in Singapore
TWP 10 9 8 7 6 5 4 3 2 1

Red Sings from Treetops

a year in colors

by Joyce Sidman

Illustrated by Pamela Zagarenski

Houghton Mifflin Books for Children
Houghton Mifflin Harcourt
Boston 2009

SPRING

In SPRING,
Red sings
from treetops:
cheer-cheer-cheer,
each note dropping
like a cherry
into my ear.

Red turns
the maples feathery,
sprouts in rhubarb spears;
Red squirms on the road
after rain.

Green is new
in spring. Shy.
Green peeks from buds,
trembles in the breeze.
Green floats through rain-dark trees,
and glows, mossy-soft, at my feet.
Green drips from tips of leaves
onto Pup's nose.

In spring,
even the rain tastes Green.

Yellow slips goldfinches
their spring jackets.
Yellow shouts with light!

In spring,
Yellow and **Purple** hold hands.
They beam at each other
with bright velvet faces.
First flowers,
first friends.

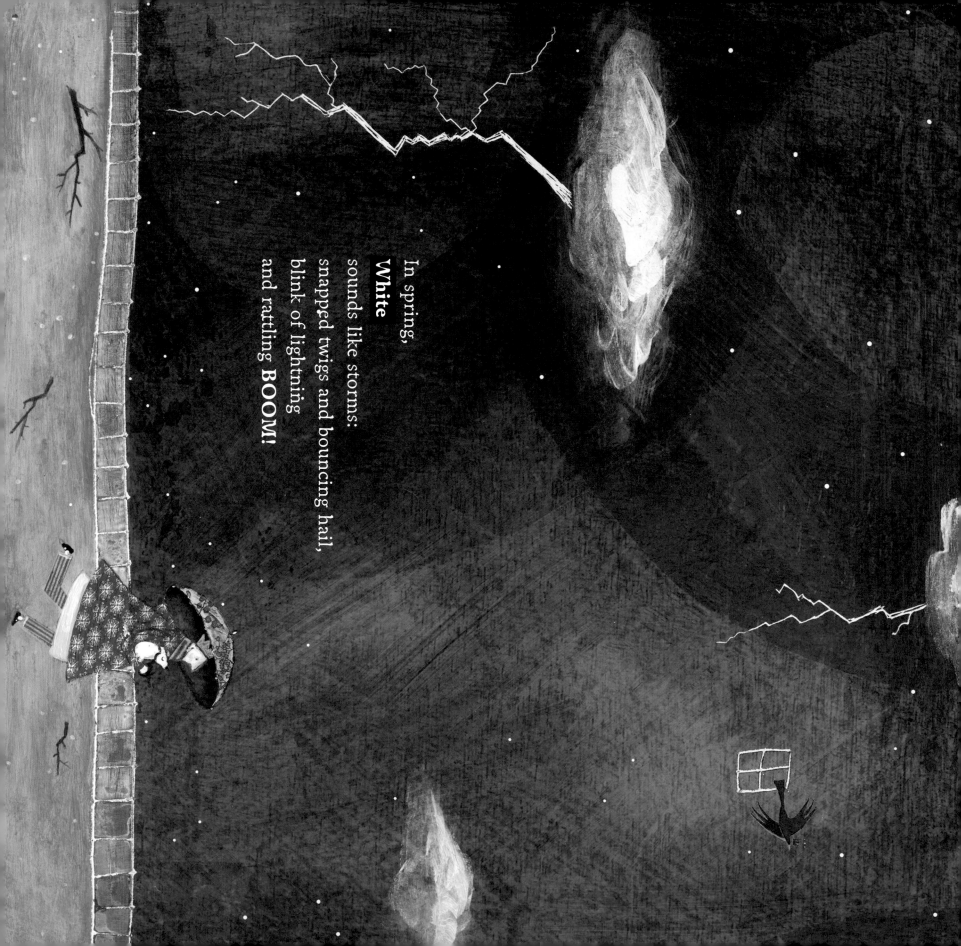

In spring,
White
sounds like storms:
snapped twigs and bouncing hail,
blink of lightning
and rattling **BOOM!**

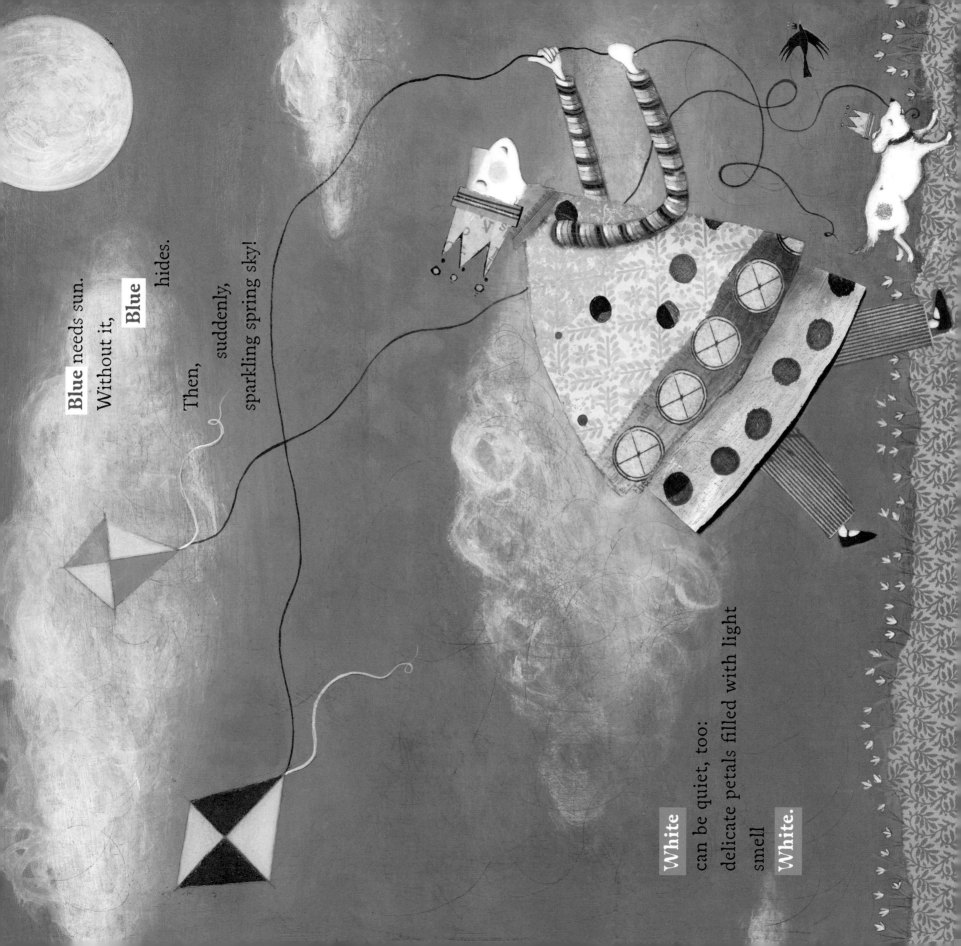

Blue needs sun.
Without it, **Blue**
hides.

Then,
suddenly,
sparkling spring sky!

White
can be quiet, too:
delicate petals filled with light
smell
White.

And here,
in secret places,
peeps **Pink:**
hairless,
featherless,
the color of
new
things.

SUMMER

In SUMMER,
White clinks in drinks.

Yellow melts
everything it touches . . .
smells like butter,
tastes like salt.

Red darts, jags,
　　　hovers;
a blur of wings,
a sequined throat.

Red whispers
along my finger
with little
beetle feet.

Green is queen
in summer.
Green trills from trees,
clings to Pup's knees,
covers all with leaves,
leaves, leaves!
How can Green be
so many different Greens?

And where is **Blue**?
Humming, shimmering,
snoozing in the lazy haze.
Dancing on water
with *Yellow* and **Green**.
In summer,
Blue grows new names:
turquoise,
azure,
cerulean.

Purple pours
into summer evenings
one shadow at a time,
so slowly
I don't notice until
hill,
   house,
      book in my hand,
  and Pup's
      Brown spots
are all
     Purple.

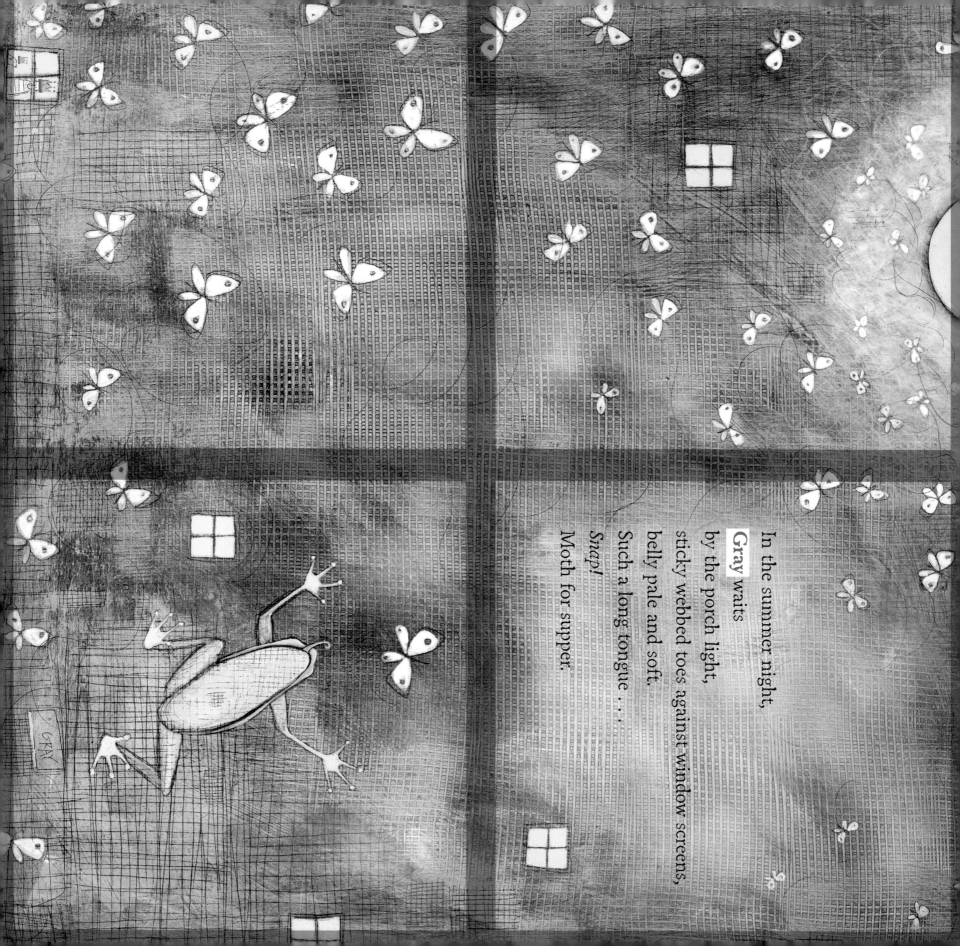

In the summer night,

Gray waits
by the porch light,
sticky-webbed toes against window screens,
belly pale and soft.
Such a long tongue . . .
Snap!
Moth for supper.

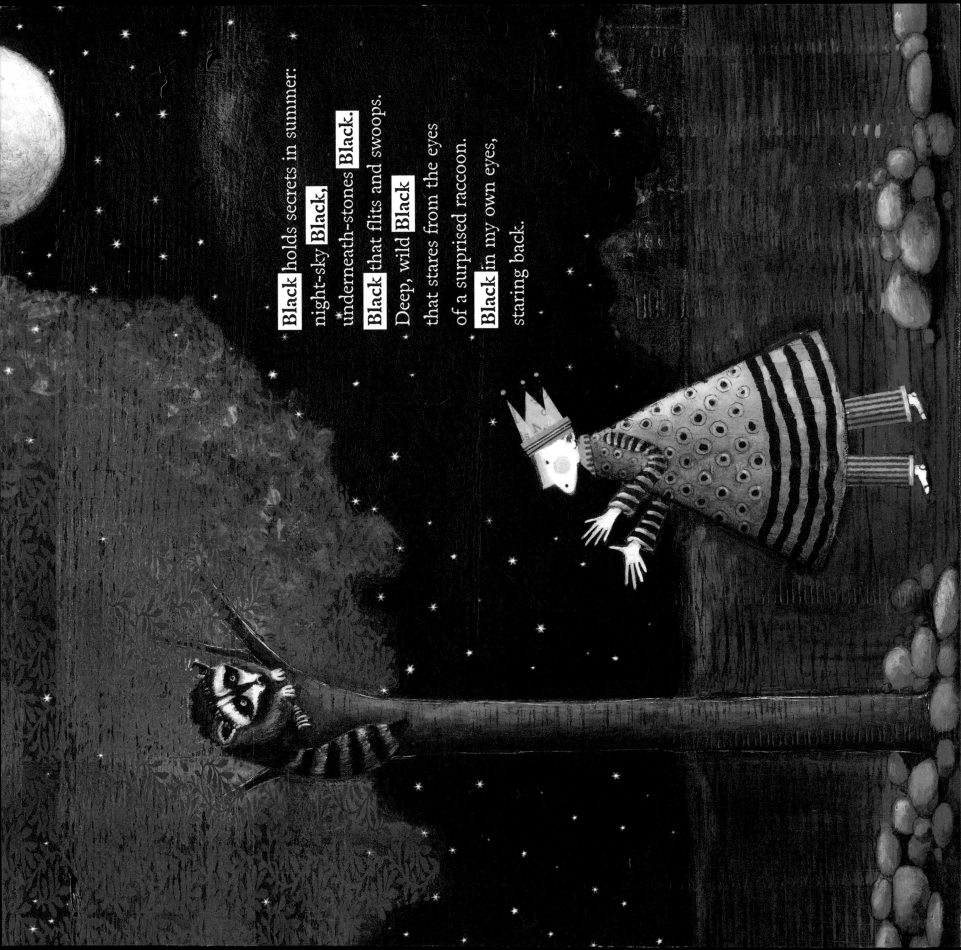

Black holds secrets in summer:
night-sky **Black**,
underneath-stones **Black**.
Black that flits and swoops.
Deep, wild **Black**
that stares from the eyes
of a surprised raccoon.
Black in my own eyes,
staring back.

FALL

In FALL,
Green is tired,
dusty,
crisp around the edges.
Green sighs with relief:
I've ruled for so long.
Time for Brown to take over.

Brown,
fat and glossy,
rises in honking flocks.
Brown rustles and whispers underfoot.
Brown gleams in my hand:
a tiny round house,
dolloped with roof.

Red splashes fall trees,
seeps into
every vein
of every five-fingered leaf.
Red swells
on branches bent low.
Red: crisp, juicy
crunch!

In fall,
Yellow grows wheels
and lumbers
down the block,
blinking:
Warning—classrooms ahead.

Fall smells
Purple:
old leaves, crushed berries,
squishy plums with worms in them.
Purple: the smell
of all things
mixed together.

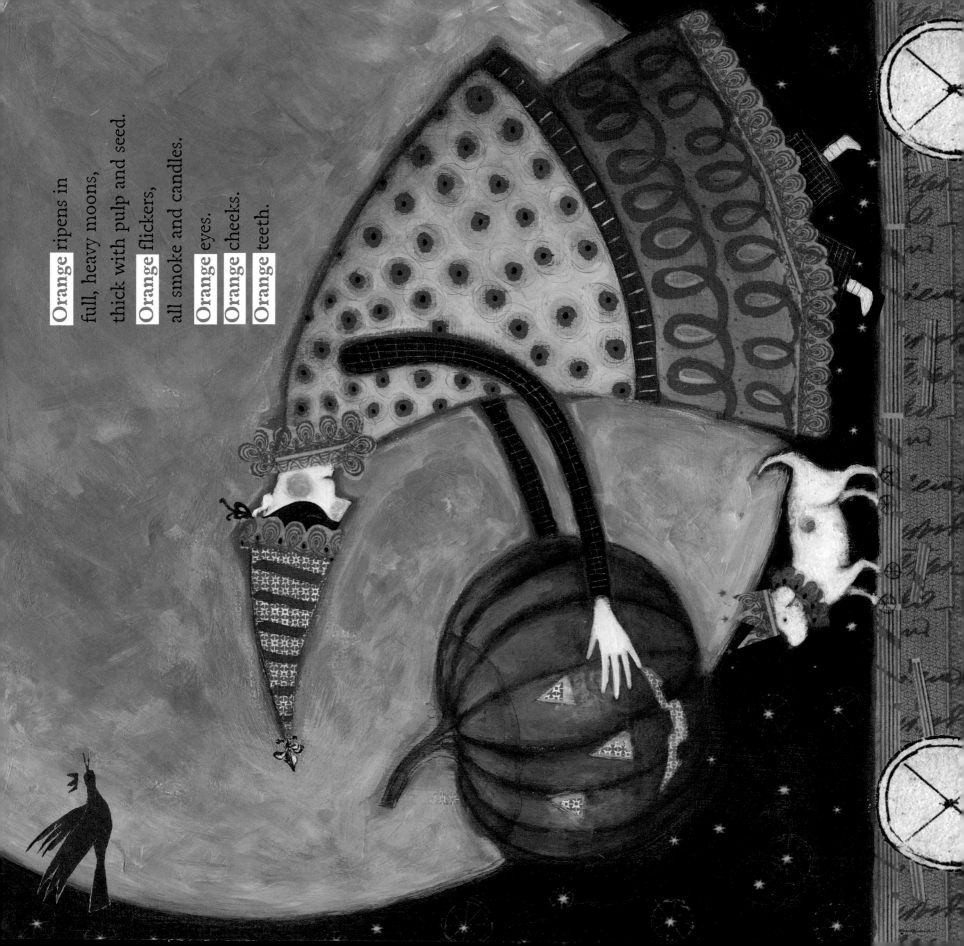

Orange ripens in
full, heavy moons,
thick with pulp and seed.
Orange flickers,
all smoke and candles.
Orange eyes.
Orange cheeks.
Orange teeth.

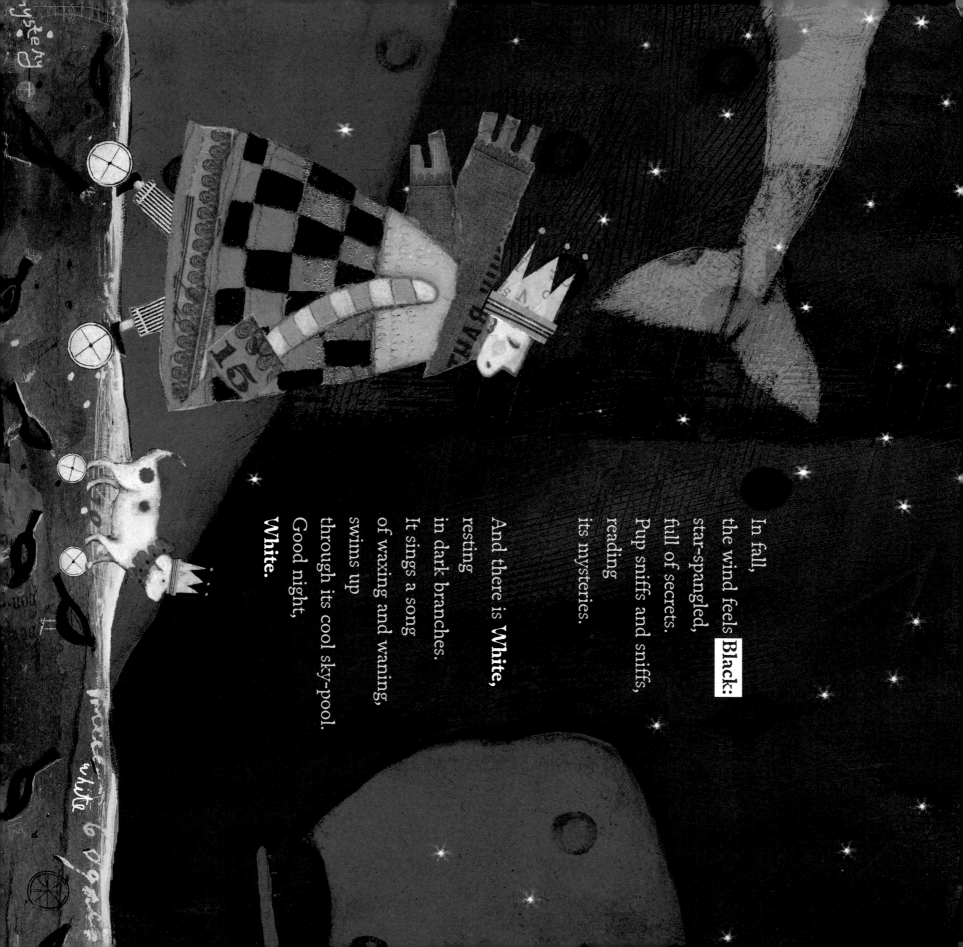

In fall,
the wind feels **Black:**
star-spangled,
full of secrets.
Pup sniffs and sniffs,
reading
its mysteries.

And there is **White,**
resting
in dark branches.
It sings a song
of waxing and waning,
swims up
through its cool sky-pool.
Good night,
White.

WINTER

In the WINTER dawn,
Pink blooms
powder-soft
over pastel hills.

Pink prickles:
warm fingers
against cold cheeks.

Blue breathes,
deep and lustrous overhead:
a glimmering dark
that slowly   turns   light.

Below,
Blue smiles
from shadows
amongst the White.

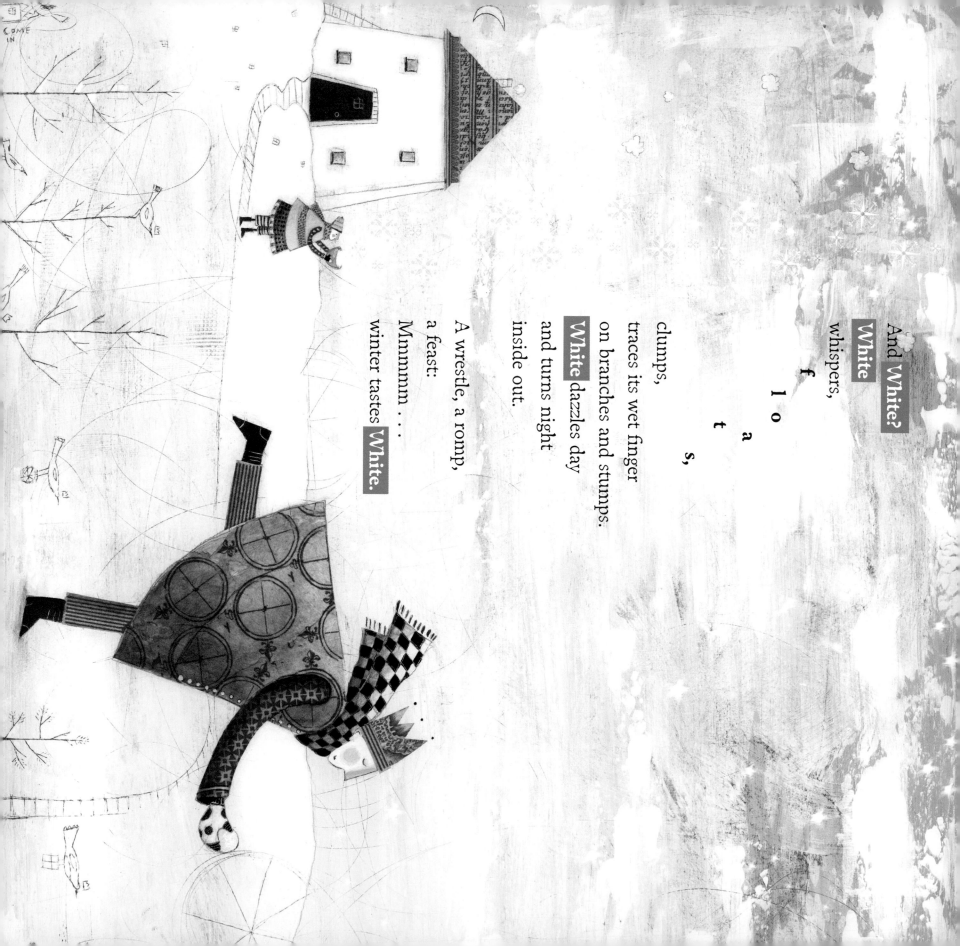

And White?

White
whispers,
White

f
l o
a
t
s,

clumps,
traces its wet finger
on branches and stumps.
White dazzles day
and turns night
inside out.

A wrestle, a romp,
a feast:
Mmmmm . . .
winter tastes White.

Against White,
Black seems **blacker:**
Black tree bones
in a pearled sky.

In the winter woods,
Gray and Brown
hold hands.
Their brilliant sisters—
Red, **Orange**, and **Yellow**—
have all gone home.
Gray and Brown sway shyly,
the only beauties left.

Where is Green in winter?
Green darkens, shrinks,
stiffens into needles.
Green waits
in the hearts of trees,
feeling
the earth
turn.

And **Red?**
Red beats inside me:
thump-thump-thump-thump.
Red glows
in the strengthening sun.

Red hops to treetops,
fluffs its feathers
against the cold.

Cheer-cheer-cheer,
it begins to sing:
and
each note drops
like a cherry
into
my
ear.